To my children

ISBN-13:978-1493749072
ISBN-10:1493749072

BUBBLES DAY

Written By
Ally Nathaniel

Illustrated By
Anahit Aleksanyan

Here is Bubbles

Do you know what bubbles loves the most?

Is it ice cream?

NO!

Is it the beach?

NO!

Is it dancing?

NO! NO! NO!

What Bubbles loves the best of all is bubbles.

She loves watching them.
She loves catching them.
She loves blowing them.

Today is the first time Bubbles will be blowing bubbles all by herself.

Bubbles is so excited!

So what does Bubbles need to do now? That's right, she needs to dip and blow!

"Like this?"

Bubbles asked?

Yes! Dip and blow. But Bubbles blew too hard and the bubble went POP!

Keep trying Bubbles
you can do it.
Blow gently,
you know how.

Bigger!

Bigger!

Great job!
You did it Bubbles!

"I did it!"
Bubbles said with
pride, as she
watched the bubble
fly away.

Other Books by Ally Nathaniel

Quick Order Form

Fax orders: 612-241-4463. Send this form.

Telephone orders: Call 973-826-2020.
Have your credit card ready

@ **Email orders:** Ally@AllyNathaniel.com

Please send the following books. I understand that I may return any of them for a full refund-for any reason, no question asked.

_____

_____

Please send more FREE information on:

☐Other Books ☐ Speaking/Seminars ☐ Consulting

Name_____
Address_____
City:_____ State: _____ Zip: _____
Telephone_____
Email address_____
sales Tax: Please add 7% sales tax.
Shipping by air: U.S.: $4.00 for first book and $2.00 for each aditional product. International: $9.00 first book; $5.00 for each additional product (estimate).

42211573R00024

Made in the USA
San Bernardino, CA
28 November 2016